The
TURKEY that
Ate My Father

The TURKEY that Ate My Father

Dean Marney

AN
APPLE
PAPERBACK

SCHOLASTIC INC.
New York Toronto London Auckland Sydney

ISBN 0-590-47730-7

12 11 10 9 8 7 6 5 4 3 2   5 6 7 8 9/9 0/0

Printed in the U.S.A.   40

First Scholastic printing, October 1995

For
Luke

1

What are you grateful for? You could be grateful that you don't have a boogerhead brother like I do. You could also be grateful that your family isn't as weird as mine is.

My dad says, "Trust your instincts, Lizzie. Listen for that still, quiet voice inside you that knows the right thing to do."

I should've listened more and sooner last Thanksgiving. You remember Thanksgiving, don't you? It's the holiday where you're supposed to be grateful and eat yourself silly.

My family *looks* normal from the outside, but looks can be deceiving. For real, my mother (because she's gone back to school — again) has decided we don't have time for TV. She went temporarily insane and canceled our cable subscription. She put our two TV's in the storage closet. Luckily, my dad got wigged out because she hadn't even asked him what he thought.

My dad said he was calling to get the cable restored immediately.

He said, "I can't believe you did this. Do you realize how hard it is to get the cable people to come out and restore cable? It'll take forever. It'll probably be easier to start our own television station."

My mom said, "We watch too much TV. It takes up too much of our time. I'm not getting enough help. We're not getting the things done we need to, and TV makes people stupid."

"Excuse me," my dad replied, "I live here, too. Thanksgiving is coming and I want to be able to watch the games."

"You can listen to them on the radio," my mom said.

"Dad," Booger asked, "when we start our own TV station, can I have my own show?"

"Not now, Booker," my dad answered.

I whispered to Booger, "You are such an idiot."

"You're not being reasonable," my dad said to my mom. "I know you're upset about school, but these kinds of things need to be our decision, not just yours. I feel like you're just looking at the things that aren't done and not seeing the things that are getting done."

I wanted to scream, "Thank you, Dad!"

Then my mother looked like she might start crying. She apologized. She admitted that being back in school was making her nuts. She didn't know how she was going to get everything done.

I then knew what was coming. I was going to be part of the solution to this problem. It never fails.

I said, "I think we should just eat out more, maybe every night. Or how about we hire a housekeeper?"

They didn't even listen to me. My mom and dad decided that the solution was that we all had to pitch in and do even more around the house. That means that I, Lizzie, had to become even more a slave than I already am. They put a list of jobs and the people who had to do them on the laundry room door.

I looked at the list. Then I looked at my mom and dad. They were both smiling like they'd done something I'd really think was great.

"Well?" my mother said to me.

Now, what do you do in this situation? Do you tell the truth? Do you tell them that you aren't running a janitorial service in your spare time? Do you tell them that there are child labor laws to protect people like me from unfair labor practices? Do you just keep your big mouth shut knowing that *anything* you say is probably going to be used against you?

"What does Booger — I mean Booker — have to do?" I asked.

Booger is my little brother. His name is Booker, but so what? He's a boogerhead if you ever met one.

"Elizabeth," my mother said.

She only calls me Elizabeth when we're with relatives who have forgotten that I exist or when I'm in trouble.

"Elizabeth," she said again, "I wish you wouldn't call him that. How many times do I have to ask you?"

"Sorry," I said.

"Booker has things to do on this list," my dad finally answered.

"But," I said, "he has half as much as I do."

"That's because you're the oldest. The oldest has the privilege of taking on more responsibility," said my mother.

I was in shock. I wondered who made that rule up.

"It's unfair," I said.

I could tell my mother was going to lose it again. Her upper lip was trembling.

"Phil?" she said.

Phil is my dad.

"Phil, I have a paper due tomorrow. I don't have time for this right now. Would you deal with this issue?"

She went in to work on the computer.

"Liz," he said. "Give us a break. You are the oldest. Your mom's not going to school forever.

We just have to cut her some slack. You can help out, can't you?"

"Yes, but it isn't fair," I said.

"Life is lots of things, Lizzie, but it isn't fair. Be grateful for what you have."

"Well, can we at least have TV back?" I said.

"Yes," my dad answered, "I'll go call right now. Why don't you get started on the list."

"I've got homework to do," I said.

"Do that first," he said, "then work on the list."

He left the room.

The first job with my name on it was "vacuum the basement."

"No way," I said.

The next job was "sweep the garage."

"You have got to be kidding," I said. "It's freezing out there."

Before I got totally depressed I went to my room to start on my homework. One of my assignments was to think of one hundred things that I was grateful for. It was going to be a toughie.

I chewed on my pencil for awhile. I could hear Booger practicing the piano. It wasn't a very pretty sound. I could smell something rotten. The garbage in my room needed taking out.

I wrote, "I'm sort of grateful I'm not in jail."

2

People tell me I have my father's eyes. We have the same shape of eyes — weird shaped; and the same color — sort of a gray. I have to tell you, before we go any further, that I like my dad. I mean, he drives me totally insane, but you know what I mean. Even though he gets mad at me, I always feel like he's going to stand up for me.

My dad is like, so predictable. I mean, he's kind of unpredictable but that's what is so predictable about him. I can usually trust him to totally embarrass me. He has absolutely no problem with yelling my name through an entire store or on a street or anywhere, until I just want to die.

I'd know him anywhere — and not just because he's my dad. He's kind of unique. Even if you dressed him up in a costume, I'd know him. He did that once. He was dressed up as Santa Claus for a Christmas party and, even though I was little, I knew it was him in five seconds.

Anyway, I guess my mom and dad kind of continued their conversation about the stuff getting done around the house. As part of the new plan to give my mother more time to get her schoolwork done, my dad was going to help more with putting together Thanksgiving dinner. It was that or cancel it.

"It won't be Thanksgiving unless it's at our house," said my dad.

Everyone always comes to our place for Thanksgiving. It's a tradition. Every relative we have (and then some) has been coming to our house since I was a baby.

"That's fine," said my mother, "but I'll need more help. I'll need people to take some responsibility."

So my mother wanted *more* help. It wasn't like we hadn't done anything before. I've helped a lot. It's the truth. I guess this year we were supposed to help *more*?

"I can help," my dad volunteered. "I can help cook."

I thought, This should be fun.

One of the unique things about my dad is that he can't cook and is a total vegetarian. He eats fruit, vegetables, and grains but no meat. He eats no beef, chicken, fish, and no turkey. Trust me on this, he shouldn't cook. But my mother went back to her schoolwork.

7

I said, "Dad, we *are* having turkey for Thanksgiving?"

"Lizzie," is all he said.

I wanted to tell him that wasn't an answer. I was worried. He had a funny look on his face. He was planning something and I didn't like it.

He said, "I've heard of people sculpting a turkey out of lentil loaf or tofu."

"Dad!" I screamed.

"I'm kidding, Liz," he said. "We'll use brown rice."

I slugged him — gently.

"You are kidding, aren't you?" I asked

"I'm going to need your help, Liz," he said. "The whole gang is coming here again for dinner and your mother has three papers due and a midterm exam. We have to shop, cook, and get the house ready."

I wanted to say, "I'm not vacuuming the basement," but didn't.

"Booker will help, too," said my dad.

"How?" I asked.

"Lizzie," he said, "all sorts of ways."

I gave him my "I don't believe you" look. I tried to look like someone who had just been told that Elvis had been spotted in their front yard. It was wasted. He was staring past me into space.

"Now what should we do first to help your mom?" he said. "It's Monday, so we'll go shopping tomorrow, start cooking Wednesday night, and throw it on the table in time for dinner on Thursday. It'll be a snap."

"You could start by calling Aunt Debbie and see what she's bringing," I said. "That's what mom always does first. You have to call everyone and see what they're bringing."

"Why?" my dad asked.

"Dad," I said, "it's just what you do. You have to call everyone and see what they're bringing and you have to tell them how good their stuff was last year."

He said, "But I don't remember what they brought last year. How can I remember? How could they remember? Don't they have more important things to think about?"

"Dad," I sighed, "I'm just trying to help. I was just telling you what Mom does."

"But that's a waste of time. They'll bring what they want anyway, won't they?"

I shrugged my shoulders. "I really don't know," I answered.

Booger came into the room.

"Are we talking about Thanksgiving?" he said.

"*We* are," I said.

"I am, too," he said.

I looked at my dad and said, "Whatever."

Booger said, "I would like to make a suggestion."

He stood and looked at us for about an hour.

"So?" I said.

"Why don't we have pizza?" he said.

"It's Thanksgiving," I said. "You have turkey and dressing on Thanksgiving. It's the law."

"It isn't either," he said.

"Well, almost," I said.

"Booker," said my dad, "we're going to go pretty traditional."

"I'll help," said Booger.

"Excuse me," I said. "With what?"

"Thanksgiving dinner," said Booger.

I wanted to say, "Yes, and pigs can fly," but instead I said, "How?"

He said, "I'll do the decorations."

I snorted.

"That's the spirit." My dad smiled. "Booger will do the decorations. This will be a snap."

"I can imagine," I said.

"Lizzie" — my dad stopped smiling — "I need you to be positive."

Then for no reason, just out of the blue, I got this funny feeling. I felt like something was going to happen. I couldn't tell if it was a good thing or a bad thing. I felt something in my stomach and it felt like something was going to happen.

I stood there a second, sort of in shock, and then said, "What?"

He repeated, "I need you to be positive."

"Fine," I said, "but if — "

"No 'but ifs,' " he said, "nothing but positives."

I could hear him but I wasn't really listening.

I was distracted by something. It was a smell or something or maybe it was the lights. Something was different.

I asked my dad, "Do you feel something?"

"Like what?"

"I don't know. I can't describe it," I said and I shivered. "Is there a window open? I feel a breeze."

"Lizzie," he said, "don't get sick on me. We need you."

I shook myself and snapped out of it.

"I'm fine," I said. "I just felt weird for a second."

"What do you think of my brussels sprouts cooked in orange juice?" asked my dad.

"Really?" I said.

"My dilled potatoes cooked with apples?"

"Dad," I tried to tell him, "this is about turkey and dressing and mashed potatoes and gravy and pumpkin pie. Who is going to make the pies?"

"I could do it," said my dad. "How hard could it be?"

I said, "I think you'd better start calling everyone to see what they're going to bring. Push pies."

3

My dad took my advice. Well, he checked with my mom first, who thought it was a great idea for him to do what she did every year anyway. He got on the phone and called everyone. He did great. I even heard him asking people to bring pies.

Everyone he talked to asked him if we were having turkey.

"I'll think about it," is all he said.

I was supposed to be working on the grocery list. My mom came into the kitchen to make some popcorn in the air popper.

I said, "Can I have some?"

"Sure," she said and gave me a bowl.

There was no butter on it.

"Mom," I said, "there's no butter on this."

"Lizzie," she sighed, "butter is fat and fat is bad. It tastes good plain."

"Mom," I said, "fat tastes good."

"Think of your health," said my mom.

"How about some salt?" I said.

"Are you kidding?" said my mom. "Do you want water retention?"

She looked at the clock.

"Oh, no," she said. "I should be twice as far as I am now. Love you, Lizzie."

With that she ran back into the spare bedroom where her desk and school stuff were.

"Hi, Mom. Bye, Mom," I said, while I melted some butter in the microwave.

I'm into health, don't get me wrong, but sometimes my parents go too far. I mean, plain popcorn just tastes so plain that I don't know why you would even bother to eat it. I had to add something to it. I didn't use a lot of butter. I did add just a little salt, too.

My list didn't look too complete, yet. I had written down only four things. I listed olives, pickles, cranberry jelly, and whipped cream for the pies.

My dad was between phone calls.

"It's a start, Liz," he said, looking over my shoulder.

"Do you think we should have guacamole and chips as an appetizer?" I asked.

"Too much fat," my dad said. "How about some salsa and we'll bake our own chips by cutting up and baking some corn tortillas?"

"Dad, it wouldn't be the same," I said.

"That's probably good," said my dad.

He wouldn't leave so I had to write down corn tortillas and salsa.

"Good," said my dad. "Now where was I? I have to call crazy Aunt Mary."

We have to call her crazy because I have two Aunt Marys. Besides, the first one is pretty crazy. She's kind of noisy and dyes her hair strange colors and can fix cars. She also has a million cats and dogs.

She'd bring something weird to Thanksgiving dinner. One year she was supposed to bring salad and she brought pistachio pudding instead. Another year she was supposed to bring rolls and she brought these giant cinnamon rolls that filled your whole plate.

One year she came to dinner dressed in black leather. She drove up to the house on a motorcycle with a guy named Spike. Another year she wore a floor-length pink evening gown, including long gloves that she bought at a yard sale. It stunk of mothballs. She didn't iron it and it was ripped in the back. You could see her purple slip.

Other than that, the dress was kind of cool in a weird sort of way. That year she brought three of her dogs with her and my grandmother said they had to stay in the garage. Those dogs barked and howled until I thought we'd all go crazy.

My mother likes her but she always says to my

dad, "Don't you ever say anything about my side of the family."

Crazy Aunt Mary feels sorry for me. Whenever she hears my parents ragging on me, especially about what I'm wearing or what I'm eating, she says, "You need to come live with me. You can wear whatever you want and eat whatever you want."

Sometimes I'm desperate, but I guess I'm not *that* desperate.

Booger came into the kitchen. I figured he smelled the popcorn. I wasn't going to give him any of mine.

"What do you want?" I asked.

"Lizzie," my dad said, holding his hand over the telephone mouthpiece, "talk nice to him."

"What do you want — please?" I said.

"Nothing," said Booger. "I need to talk to dad about something."

"What something?" I asked.

My dad has this thing about the word "something" and now I'm starting to do it. It makes him super crazy when he asks you what you're watching on TV and you answer, "Something." If he asks you what you are doing and you answer "Something," he goes psycho.

He says, "There is no program on TV called 'Something,' " or "How do you play 'Something'? What is this 'Something' specifically in detail?"

It's pretty hard to tell him, "I don't want you to know because you're going to yell at me for doing it and if I was doing something that you wanted me to do I would be happy to tell you."

Sometimes parents can be a little slow to catch on.

"Something what?" I repeated at Booger.

"None of your business," he said. "I'm talking to Dad."

"He's going to be on the phone forever so you might as well tell me so I can decide whether you should tell him or not."

"Are you nuts?" he asked.

"Is this a trick question? You are asking me if I'm nuts?" I said. "Do I live with you?"

My mother yelled down the hall, "Can you two please not fight?"

"Now see what you've done?" I said.

Booger had something in his hands. He was trying to hide it from me. I don't know why but I was dying to know what it was.

"What do you have in your hands?" I said.

"Nothing," said Booger.

"That," I said, "is definitely something."

"It is none of your business," he said.

I was going to grab it from him but my dad got off the phone.

"Dad," said Booger, "can I order this giant folding turkey decoration?"

My dad asked, "How much is it?"

"Free," said Booger.

"Huh?" I said.

"And it says there is immediate delivery," said Booger. "It says so in this catalog."

He handed the catalog to my dad.

My dad read the cover, *"Ralph's Genuine Thanksgiving Catalog.* Guaranteed to make you grateful. Order through our toll-free number. Cost and shipping are free. Be grateful. It's all free."

"Ralph's?" I asked. "Did you say Ralph's?"

I could feel the electrical impulses in my brain trying to make connections.

I thought, Could it be the same Ralph of "Ralph's Magic Christmas Trees?" "Ralph's Halloween Store?" I think I know this guy.

Suddenly I felt my brain go fuzzy. I was trying to remember something specific about this Ralph character, but I couldn't make my brain work. My thoughts were swirling around like they were in a blender on high. At that moment, I would have had trouble telling you my name.

I couldn't make sense of anything. It all seemed like mush. The only thought I could hang on to was that I'd run into Ralph before and Ralph was trouble. I could remember that he was a strange man and every time he came into my life, very strange things happened.

"Well," said my dad, "I don't think it will get here in time."

Booger was like totally disappointed.

"It's a paper turkey," I said to him.

"It's giant," he said. "It says it is so big it's magical."

"Oh, all right," my dad gave in. "What can it hurt? Nothing is free though. I wonder what the catch is. You'd better let me order it."

My dad dialed the number. It was 1-800-TURKEYS. He talked a long time on the phone and then hung up.

"That's weird," he said. "I talked to Ralph himself. It was like he was expecting me to call. He promised me there was no catch. He's shipping it out."

Booger clapped his hands.

"Really?" I asked.

"He also said that it is really, *really* big," said my dad.

"How big?" I asked.

"He said I could never imagine a turkey could be so big," said my dad.

"What else did he say?" asked Booger.

"He said to tell Booker and especially Lizzie, 'Hello.' I guess he must have all our names on his computer. It's still weird."

I got that funny feeling again. It was the Ralph thing. The room felt like it was spinning.

"Lizzie?" My dad looked at me. "Are you okay?"

"I don't know," I answered. "I don't know."

4

I went upstairs to do my homework. Call me crazy, but I thought it would make me feel better. However, at first I couldn't find my backpack and then when I found it, I couldn't find my math book, and then I couldn't remember what else I was supposed to do.

I knew I had to do something for our history class but I'd left my notebook at school and it had all my assignments in it. I tried to remember what the teacher had said. I couldn't. I decided I was probably supposed to just read a little in my history book. That sounded good because I'd rather read than do most things.

We're studying the ancient Greeks. I don't know why, but I really like it. I like all the stories about the heroes and the gods and goddesses. I think their clothes looked cool, too. They looked super comfortable.

One thing I don't like about them was their attitude toward women. It was like women were the property of their fathers and their husbands. Sorry, it wouldn't have happened to me.

It probably wouldn't have mattered because I would've been a slave. I would've been vacuuming the basement and sweeping the garage and everything else anyone could think of.

I can hear myself now. "Dust the entire Parthenon inside and out this afternoon? Is that all?"

A teacher heard me griping to my sort-of friend Louise about my parents making me do everything and he said, "Don't knock it. There's good money in janitorial work."

"Not at my house," I said after he left.

One of the Greek myths is about Hercules and how he had to do these twelve tasks because he ticked-off this goddess Hera. One of his tasks was that he had to clean the stables of this king. The stables hadn't been cleaned in thirty years. Get this, a herd of three thousand oxen lived in the stable.

We are talking about some serious piles of manure and Hercules was supposed to clean it all up in one day. Even though he was totally amazing, he was depressed because it was a cleaning job no one could do in that little time. I do not want to even think about the number of flies and the smell of the place. It would have to be way beyond the P.U. stage.

Lucky for Hercules there were two rivers flowing close by. To solve the problem and clean the stables, Hercules just dug a ditch and diverted the rivers into the stables. The rivers washed them out in no time at all. All the crap went downstream.

Now, that was great for Hercules, but what about the people who lived downstream? Excuse me, Hercules, but have you ever heard of water pollution? Would you want your water supply filled with thirty years worth of ox manure? I don't think so. I'll bet the fish didn't think it was such a great idea, either.

If you ask me, he wasn't always too creative in solving his problems. He was kind of big on solving every problem in life by killing it. For example, he was beating this huge lion with a club because the lion had the annoying habit of eating everyone. Well, Hercules was having trouble because the lion's skull was so thick, the club couldn't hurt him. Instead of having a clue and rethinking the whole thing, Hercules's creative solution was to switch to strangling him.

I mean, maybe the lion had a thorn in its foot? Did he stop to think of that? Did he consider that maybe the lion was hungry and maybe they should try feeding him? No, Hercules just beat and strangled him.

Consider the time when he had to go into this swamp and kill the Hydra. Actually, it was probably a good thing that he got rid of the Hydra. The Hydra was this monster dragon with nine heads. Hercules cut off the Hydra's heads with his sword, but every time he'd slice one off they'd grow back instantly; and this time where there used to be one head there were now two. It starts sounding like a math story problem doesn't it? *Question:* If Hercules knocked off all nine original heads plus two new ones, how many were left? *Answer:* Too many!

Well, to destroy this monster he tied it up and burned all of its heads off except one, which he buried under a rock. I guess there was one head that you couldn't kill no matter what, so you have to bury it.

I guess I don't like Hercules that much. He was strong and cute, but it doesn't seem like he thought everything through very well. Not that I do every time, either, but I've never done anything major like he did.

He also killed the queen of the Amazons and stole her girdle. Everyone thought that was like seriously funny but then the teacher said it was like a belt. The Amazons were a nation of women only. They didn't let guys in. They sound smart.

Today we were studying a guy named Theseus. Pronounce it anyway you want; I do. He was sort of cool and sort of a jerk because of what he did to his so-called new girlfriend.

I asked our teacher whether all the heroes were like both good and also jerks.

She said, "Totally. They were always heroic but

also made tragic mistakes that usually changed peoples lives in huge ways."

"Why?" I asked. "Why couldn't they just do good stuff?"

"Can you think of a reason?" she asked.

"I don't know," I said.

"If they did only 'good stuff' and made only perfect decisions, would they be human? Could it be that overcoming their mistakes and the ways they handled the bad stuff around them is what truly made them heroic?" she asked me.

"I guess," I said.

Anyway, Theseus was going to see his dad who didn't know what he looked like. Theseus's dad was under the spell of this witch named Medea who wanted to get rid of Theseus when he came to visit. When Theseus came to the palace, his dad didn't recognize him.

Witchy Medea told his dad that Theseus was someone else and that his dad should poison him because, if he didn't, Theseus was going to poison him first. It was a total lie but the king believed it.

She talked him into poisoning Theseus, but just when Theseus was going to drink the poison his dad recognized him. They then got rid of Medea, instead. I think that was a good choice.

Well, Theseus's dad was fighting with this other king, called King Minos, who was going to destroy his kingdom unless seven young men and seven young women were sent to him every year. King Minos would take the fourteen people down under his palace into the labyrinth, which was such an incredible maze that no one could ever get out of it.

Down in his labyrinth was a half-man and half-bull named the Minotaur, who like starved all year and then binged on the fourteen men and women for breakfast, lunch, and dinner. I'll bet they went ladies first, too.

Theseus told his dad he wanted to be one of those sent to King Minos because he was going to kill the Minotaur and stop this weird sacrifice number. At first his dad didn't want him to do it but then Theseus talked him into it.

I can just see me telling my dad, "Please let me go. I'll kill the monster and be right back."

"Sure, honey," he'd answer. "Have a nice day."

I don't think so.

Theseus goes on a ship with the hysterical people who think they're going to be Minotaur snackies. He gets on shore and King Minos's daughter Ariadne falls like totally in love at first sight. He must have been super cute or something or maybe she was desperate. We don't know.

Anyway, she doesn't want him to be killed so she gives him a sword and some golden thread so he can kill the Minotaur and find his way back out of the labyrinth by following the thread. Well,

Theseus has no trouble in the labyrinth. He murders the Minotaur like it's no big deal. Then he follows the thread that he had tied at the entrance to the labyrinth, gets out, hops a boat with the rest of the people he came with, and takes Ariadne with him because her dad was going to be ballistic with her when he found out what she'd done. Besides, Theseus was probably acting like he loved her, too.

Here is where he screwed up big time. On the way home they stopped at this island. He had a dream where one of the goddesses told him to leave Ariadne there. So he wakes up and sneaks away with the rest of the people and leaves Ariadne on this island. The only thing I can figure is she must have been a heavy sleeper or real tired.

Now, wasn't he grateful? Here is this woman who saves his life. He owes her. She gave up everything to save him. What thanks does she get?

She doesn't even get a dumb card or some cheap candy. He dumps her on some stupid island after one little dream and sails away. What is she supposed to do, swim home? Guys can be so inconsiderate.

To make matters worse, he was supposed to change the sails of the boat from black to white so his dad could see from a distance that Theseus had been successful and was still alive. He forgot. Stupid! If he wouldn't have dogged Ariadne, she probably could've reminded him.

"Theseus, did you change the sails?"

"Thanks, Ariadne, I almost forgot. You have saved me once again."

Well, he didn't change the sails and his dad was so depressed he killed himself.

I just want to scream at both of them, "You idiots!"

Theseus was the hero because he killed the Minotaur but he lost the woman who really loved him and he lost his father.

My teacher says, "This is tragedy. These stories are about fate and how bad things can happen just by being human and forgetting to do something you said you would."

I was depressed. I like these stories but they can be, well, so . . . depressing.

5

I ate lunch with Bob that day. Bob is a girl. Her real name is Roberta but everyone calls her Bob for short.

We were minding our own business, eating lunch and talking. For no reason Scott threw a wadded-up napkin at me.

Boys are so weird. I mean, girls can be weird but boys are really weird. I don't understand them.

"Do you have a problem?" I asked.

"No," Scott answered, "do you?"

Bob whispered to me, "I think he likes you."

"No way."

"Could be," said Bob. "Guys can act weird."

"No way," I said again. "He's a jerk. He's a *total* jerk. He's beyond a jerk."

He was sitting about twelve feet from us and kind of staring. It was giving me the creeps.

"See," said Bob.

"No way," I said.

27

We went outside to finish the lunch period. We barely had any time to do anything fun. By the way, does it seem like they shorten the lunch period every year? Didn't it used to be called the lunch hour? Now it's called poke your food down as fast as you can, go to the toilet, and get back to class.

Bob and I were out shooting baskets and these boys wanted to play us a game and we could've beat them but we didn't have time. The bell rang and we had to go back in.

Inside the door opposite the principal's office was this mural some class had done. It was mostly of this giant turkey. I looked at it for a second and it almost freaked me out. It was the meanest-looking thing I'd ever seen; well practically.

"Weird," I said.

"I'll say," Bob agreed.

"I wouldn't want to mess with that turkey," I said.

"Neither would I," said Bob. "Do you know what my uncle told me about turkeys? He raised them for awhile."

"What?" I asked.

"He said that they were so dumb that you had to bring them in during a rainstorm or they would stand in the rain, look up at the sky, open their mouths, and drown."

"No," I said, "really?"

"That's what he said."

"Mean and stupid," I said. "It sounds like a great combo to me."

We walked back to our classroom. We were going to practice the Thanksgiving skit we were doing for the entire school the next day. I was a pilgrim. All the girls were pilgrims.

It's a weird skit because our music teacher, Mr. Drake, let us pick our own parts. He's all hot on having us be creative. All the girls decided to be pilgrims and all the boys decided to be Native Americans. We also designed our own costumes.

Mr. Drake said, "This is a terrific skit, your creativity just shines."

The boys had all decided to take their shirts off and paint themselves, and they wanted to practice the skit with the paint on. Mr. Drake thought that would be very creative. It was.

They proceeded to creatively get paint everywhere and they were being totally strange. They painted bull's-eyes on each other and stuff that was supposed to look like tattoos, like battleships and hearts and stuff. They got the paint all over their pants.

Mr. Drake laughed and said, "I hope it washes out."

No kidding, I thought.

The girls were more sensible. We worked up these black-and-white numbers with stuff out of the costume closet. We made our own paper hats, which turned out a little different from how we thought they would. We couldn't get them exactly right. The problem was they made us look more like nuns than pilgrims.

Bob kept saying we should call the play *Little Convent on the Prairie*.

The hats weren't that bad. They just weren't that great. I'm just grateful we weren't as creative as the boys.

Marcia refused to wear black and white. Talk about being a little strange, she is. She's the bossiest girl in the world.

"I only wear pink," she said.

Everyone said, "We know."

She wears pink every day. She even wears pink shoes. She has a pink lunch sack. She's got this pink thing going.

"It's a play," I said. "You are supposed to pretend. Pretend the dress is pink."

"I don't care. I hate wearing black," she said.

"Fine," Mr. Drake said. "Be a pink pilgrim. It's very creative."

"You're going to look stupid," I whispered to her.

"I don't care," Marcia whined.

"Okay," I said.

The story was stupid enough without a pink pilgrim. It was about two pilgrims getting lost in the forest on their way to the Thanksgiving feast until the kindly Native Americans show up to lead the way. Then we all eat dinner and sing this totally stupid Thanksgiving song — and that's the end of the story.

The only good part was that we had great fake food to put on the table for the feast. We had fake corn and apples and fake tomatoes and grapes. We also had this really big, fake, plastic, cooked turkey.

When the boys finished cleaning up their paint mess, which took forever because they had it all over the floor, we did a run-through of the skit. It was bad. It was probably a disaster.

The two girls, Jane and Emily, who were supposed to be lost in the forest, were wearing high heels that were ten sizes too big for them. Jane started to fall down so she grabbed on to Emily and they both fell to the ground. Jane thought she'd broken her ankle so she had to go see the school nurse.

Then one of the guys, Tim, got allergic to the paint. He started itching and then he started breaking out in these big, blotchy-looking things. Mr. Drake had to call someone to come get him.

Mr. Drake was getting kind of strung out. He decided maybe we should be a little less creative. The high heels and the paint had to go.

I was standing at the back of the room waiting for Mr. Drake to tell us we could go change our clothes. I swear to you I was minding my own business. Mr. Drake was talking to Marcia, who thought we should videotape the skit.

He said, "I don't think that's a good idea."

Right, I thought, he doesn't want any evidence.

For some reason I happened to look over at Scott. I should never have looked at him. He saw me.

Then, for some reason, he picked up the turkey and yelled at me, "Hey, Lizzie, have some turkey!"

Then he threw the plastic turkey across the entire classroom. I was surprised, but I shouldn't have been because he is so dang wild. What I should've really been surprised at was that I actually caught the turkey. It was a great catch if I do say so myself.

Mr. Drake was at an extremely high stress level.

He said, "I don't believe what I just saw. Lizzie and Scott, to the office, now."

"What did I do?" I asked.

"Now!" he said again.

I couldn't believe I was in trouble. The only thing I did was keep the turkey from hitting the wall and probably hurting something or someone.

"Mr. Drake," I said, "I just caught it."

It didn't matter. We both got sent to the principal's office. Scott looked like he had been in a paint fight and lost, and I looked like a nun, and we were sitting on the bench outside the principal's office.

"I detest you," I said to Scott, looking at that ugly turkey mural on the wall.

We went into the principal's office.

She sighed and shook her head. "Not you two, again?"

6

Game over — we were out of the skit. It wasn't exactly justice. The principal barely asked us what happened.

"Scott threw the turkey and basically I caught it," I said.

She took one look at us in costume and said we couldn't be in the skit. She didn't even ask Scott why he threw the turkey. She didn't even let me explain that I was just trying to keep the turkey from hitting the wall.

Besides that, she said she was going to call our parents.

"For catching a turkey that you hadn't even asked to have thrown at you?" I wanted to ask.

Instead I said, "I'm sorry. Doesn't that count?"

My parents were going to have heart attacks they were going to be so mad. My mother was going to have a cow. On top of being so tense about going to school, this would probably push her over the edge.

The principal said, "I accept your apology but I also need you two not to cause this kind of problem. As I remember, you were just in here last month for throwing clay at one another."

Scott, that big creep, didn't say a word. He could've said it was all his fault. He could've taken the blame. No, he let me get totally in trouble.

We stepped out of the principal's office and I said to him, "I can't believe you did this to me."

"What do you mean?"

"You creep," I said. "You big, horrible creep. See that stupid giant turkey over on that wall?" I pointed at the turkey mural. "That's what you are."

"Gee," said Scott sarcastically, "that really hurt my feelings. Why don't you try something else?"

All of a sudden I felt like I was going to hurl. It was like, instantaneously. For some reason, I looked at the turkey at the same time. It was wavy. The feathers looked like little doors and they were opening and closing.

"Are you okay?" said Scott.

It stopped.

"I don't know," I said. "I thought I was going to throw up but now I feel a little better."

"Do you want to go back into the principal's office?" he asked.

"No way," I said. "I feel fine. I want to go change my clothes."

We started down the hall. It was the strangest

thing, though. It didn't feel quite right. It didn't feel like our school hall.

There were classroom doors but they didn't have windows in them. There was no one else in the hallway. It also didn't smell like our school. It smelled damp, like an old basement.

"Don't the classroom doors have windows in them?" I asked Scott.

"They used to," he said.

"I mean," I said, "when we came down here, didn't the doors have windows?"

"I guess they couldn't have," said Scott, looking at all the windowless doors.

We turned the corner to go down our corridor. I must have made this trip a million times. I knew how to get to my classroom.

We were in the wrong corridor. I didn't know what corridor we were in.

"Where are we?" Scott asked.

"I don't know," I said.

We kept walking, but at the end of the corridor there was another corridor. It wasn't ours, either. There were still no people.

"Try one of the doors," I said.

"I'll get in bigger trouble," Scott said.

"You should've thought of that before you threw the turkey," I said.

I reached over and tried the door. It was unlocked. I opened it expecting to find a classroom. Instead there was another corridor.

I was going to hurl for sure.

"This is weird," said Scott, "this is very weird. Our classroom is lost."

"Don't be stupid," I said. "Let's just go back to the principal's office and start over."

"Our class has to be here someplace," said Scott.

We backtracked the way we came but, when we got to the corridor where the principal's office should've been, it wasn't there.

"I don't believe this," I said. "I'm lost in my own school."

"Hey, anybody home?" yelled Scott.

"Stop it," I said. "We're going to get in bigger trouble."

However, nothing happened. No one came out into the hall.

I tried this time. I mean, I really yelled.

"Anyone home?!"

It echoed.

"Cool," said Scott.

"This is freaky," I said. "What is going on?"

Then the bell rang. I mean it super rang. I've never heard it ring like that. It was deafening. It rang so hard I could feel it vibrating through my whole body.

Suddenly all the doors burst open and there were all these kids in the hallway. We were once again standing outside the principal's office. There was that stupid turkey on the wall.

"Huh?" I said.

"What happened?" said Scott.

We stood there a little dazed.

"Didn't we try to get to our classroom?" I asked.

"I don't know," said Scott.

The principal came out of her office.

"Are you two still here? Get down to your classroom and change your clothes. I don't want to see either of you down here again. Do you hear me?"

"I think we tried," said Scott.

"Try harder," said the principal.

She turned to yell at some kids playing with the drinking fountain.

"I've got to wash this paint off," said Scott. "I'm starting to flake."

"No kidding." I said. "I've got to talk to my parents before the principal does. I've got to find a phone."

We ran down the hall until a teacher saw us and told us to slow down.

"Don't do anything stupid," I said to Scott.

7

I had to call my dad. I figured that if I called him, he could call my mom and prepare her. I thought that if I could talk to him first then maybe no one would be mad at me and we could forget this whole thing.

"Ya, right," I said to myself.

School was just out for the day and there was a line a mile long at the one pay phone in the whole school. Everyone was trying to get their parents to come get them so they wouldn't have to ride the bus. I got in line.

I waited patiently for a long time. I waited so long that I was going to miss my bus. This stupid boy at the phone kept dialing the wrong number. Everyone went crazy every time he redialed. I swear his fingers had to be exhausted from all the times he pressed the buttons.

I couldn't take it anymore. I went up to the phone.

"Listen, you moron," I said. "Give me that

phone. If you don't know your number, go look it up."

The kids in the line cheered.

The loudspeaker said, "The buses are leaving. Everyone please board your bus."

"You've got to be kidding," I said.

Now I was going to miss my bus *and* get in deep trouble. I started to use the phone. I was calling my dad at work.

Everyone, I mean everyone, in line started yelling, "Cuts! Cuts!"

I yelled back, "It's an emergency."

Mr. Brown, our librarian, happened to be right there.

He said, "Lizzie, get to the back of the line please. We don't cut. We have rules and we follow them."

"Great," I said.

I was going to get in line and miss the bus and walk home. Then I thought I'd be in bigger trouble. Then I thought I could run away. Then I remembered I only had thirty-five cents in my pocket.

I gave up and ran out to my bus. It was getting ready to take off.

"Wait!" I yelled.

Doris, our bus driver, said, "Get your act together, Lizzie. You almost had to walk home."

Then there was only one empty seat. It was next to Booger.

"Hi, Lizzie," he said.

"Please," I said, "don't act like you know me."

The bus took off. From the back of the bus I heard turkey noises. I didn't want to turn around.

It was getting louder. Some kids in the bus were gobbling.

They were saying, "Hey, Lizzie, gobble, gobble."

Booger asked, "Why are they doing that?"

"Because they're idiots," I said.

Doris didn't make them shut up until we were practically home.

Walking from the bus stop to our house, Booger kept saying, "Turkey, turkey, gobble, gobble. Eat too much, wobble, wobble."

"Do you have to do that?" I asked him.

"No," he said, and then he did it again.

We went into the house.

"Have a nice day?" my mom asked us.

"No," I answered.

"Don't be negative, dear," my mom told me. "I got one of my papers done."

"Good," whined Booger. "Does that mean you're cooking dinner tonight?"

"Absolutely," she said, "but you guys have to help."

"I'd love to, Mom," I said, "but I have a ton of homework."

"That, I understand." My mom smiled.

"I'll help," chirped Booger, "but can I go out and play first?"

"Sure," said my mom.

I was grabbing myself an apple for a snack. I wanted chips but I knew I wouldn't get away with it.

"That's a healthy choice," said my mom. "How about a glass of water, too."

She poured me one.

"Lizzie," she said, "I'm sorry I've been so cranky. This school thing is just a little more time-consuming than I thought it was going to be. I'm trying to get it down but sometimes I get pretty overwhelmed."

I wasn't sure I should do it but she seemed like she was in a good mood. I opened my mouth and without thinking about how I was going to tell her, it came blurting out fast and high. I kind of sounded like a talking cricket. "The principal is calling you but it wasn't my fault."

"What?" she said also in an unnaturally high voice.

"Scott threw this turkey and I only caught it to keep it from hitting the wall, but I got in trouble anyway. It really wasn't my fault. Scott is just too chicken to take the blame."

"Lizzie," she said, "I don't believe this."

"I don't either," I said.

"You dad is going to flip sideways," she said.

She stood and looked at me a long time.

"Let me hear your side of the story," she said.

"That *was* my side of the story," I said.

I started to tell it to her again but the phone rang.

It was my dad.

"You won't believe what Lizzie did," said my mom.

She raised her eyebrows at me.

"Yes, again," she said. "This time she caught a turkey."

There was a pause.

She said, "I don't think it was a real turkey." She put her hand over the receiver. "Lizzie, was it a real turkey?"

"No," I said, "it was a plastic one."

"She says it was a plastic one."

I took a bite of my apple.

She went around the corner of the kitchen doorway so all I could hear was some mumbling. I wondered what wonderful punishment I was going to get. I waited for her to hang up. She came back into the kitchen.

"I want the truth," my mom said, "really."

I told her. I told her I was innocent. I told her Scott's a jerk. She didn't believe me.

8

I was insane. I kept waiting for the call. The call never came.

Every time the phone rang I jumped sixty feet. I felt like a kangaroo. My stomach was upset. I had a headache. I couldn't understand why the principal just didn't call.

My dad came home and she still hadn't called.

"You caught a turkey?" he asked.

"Lizzie caught a turkey?" Booger interrupted. "Where is it?"

"Someone threw a turkey and Lizzie caught it," said my mom.

I couldn't believe she was trying to explain it to Booger.

"It wasn't a real turkey," I said. "It was plastic and it was Scott."

"The turkey's name was Scott?" Booger asked.

"Scott is a turkey for sure, but no, the turkey didn't have a name. It was just a stupid plastic turkey that Scott decided to heave across the room. He just happened to throw it to me. I don't understand what the big deal is," I said.

"Why do you suppose he threw it to you?" asked my mom.

"I have no idea," I said. "Probably because he's weird. I don't know. He does things like that."

"Lizzie," said my dad, "I can't believe that you are completely without fault in this. It can't be all Scott's fault."

"Honest, Dad," I started crying, "I was just standing there."

"Well," he said, "we'll talk about it later."

The phone rang. It wasn't the principal — again. It was someone trying to sell my mother something.

She said, "I don't buy over the phone, thank you."

We sat down to dinner. It was totally vegetarian and healthy. It was boring. My dad loved it.

"Is there dessert?" I asked.

"No," my mother answered.

What a day, I thought.

I was trying to be good. I didn't even say anything when Booger had to tell us the story of *Chicken-Little*. You know the story — everyone does — about how this stupid chicken thinks the sky is falling because an acorn fell on her head. She runs around to all these other animals, convincing them.

They all have stupid names like Henny-Penny,

Turkey-Lurkey, and Ducky-Lucky. Booger was doing these dumb little voices for all the characters. I thought I might lose my vegetarian dinner. I couldn't wait till the fox, who wasn't a vegetarian, caught them all and ate them. I was rooting for him even though his name was Foxy-Loxy.

The stupid phone was never going to ring. I wondered what that principal was doing. I helped with the dishes.

I couldn't stand it anymore. Before I went to my room I asked, "Okay, what's my punishment?"

"Let's just wait and see," said my dad.

I wrote in my diary what a jerk Scott was and what an awful day I'd had. I tried to write down what happened when Scott and I got lost. As I wrote, it came to me how strange what happened was and how it couldn't have happened. My pen ran out of ink. That was so irritating.

I went downstairs to get another one.

My dad asked, "Liz, did you do anything on the list today?"

"Well, I've been really busy," I said.

"Liz, we've got a lot to do," he said.

The phone rang. It was for my dad. It still wasn't the principal.

Booger was sitting at the kitchen table doing something.

"What are you doing?" I asked.

"Nothing," he said.

46

He was drawing on a piece of paper. I grabbed it away from him.

"Knock it off!" he screamed. "Give it back!"

"Don't be such a big baby," I said.

"Dad!" he yelled.

"Oh, all right," I said. "Here, have it back."

He took it back.

Dad yelled, "What do you want?"

"Nothing," I answered.

Booger went back to drawing.

"You're drawing a maze, aren't you? You love mazes. Why do you always draw mazes?" I asked.

"I like mazes," he said.

It's the truth. I guess all kids like mazes. I like to do mazes. We always fight over who'll do the ones in the kids' section of the paper.

Booger once got a book of mazes that were really hard. He worked on them all the time until the book was so grubby you wanted to have it condemned. He was totally obsessed by those mazes.

My mom came in and said that Booger and I should go to bed. I looked at her like she was from Mars, but I didn't say anything. I just wished the dang principal would call, my parents would punish me, and we could get this over with.

I went to bed and I didn't think I was tired enough to go to sleep, but I did. I dreamt of Ariadne. Is that weird or what? You know, she's the woman Theseus dumped on the island because he had a bad dream.

I dreamt she was on an island. I was with her. She asked me if I wanted to go swimming. I said okay.

We started walking to the beach, but the beach was really long and our feet were burning on the sand. We ran. We ran incredibly fast and right into the ocean.

We were laughing and I was glad I had a new friend. Then a boat came and she said she was leaving. She said she was going to change her name.

She said, "You don't have to catch every turkey that gets thrown to you. People aren't always who they seem to be."

I woke up because I had to go to the bathroom. I went and then got back in bed. I tried to go back to sleep but I kept thinking of turkeys. I kept going "Turkey-Lurkey" in my head. I hate it when I do that.

9

When I got to school the next day, I was told I had to go to the principal's office.

"We're starting out good," I said.

I hated sitting outside her door looking at the turkey. I finally closed my eyes so I wouldn't have to look at it. I thought about how Scott and I couldn't find our way back to our classroom, but now that seemed like a dream.

I suddenly realized I wasn't breathing and I felt kind of sick to my stomach. I had no idea what the principal was going to do. Finally, she called me in.

"Elizabeth," she said, "you probably noticed that I didn't call your parents last night."

I didn't say anything. I was looking into her wastebasket. There was a candy bar wrapper in it. I wondered if she had eaten a candy bar for breakfast.

"I owe you an apology," she said.

That woke me up.

"After school," she continued, "Scott came back to see me and told me that it was his fault. He stated that he had decided to throw the ball — no, it wasn't a ball."

"It was a turkey," I said.

"Right," she said. "He threw a turkey across the room and you just happened to catch it."

I couldn't believe this was happening.

"So, young lady," she said, "you're off the hook. I'll write you a note to give to Mr. Drake and I will also write a note to give to your parents. I assume you told them I was calling?"

"Yes," I answered and now wished I hadn't told them.

She wrote out two notes.

"I'll see you at the play," she said.

"Thank you," I said, and then again, "thank you."

My luck had totally changed. I could've flown down the hall. I walked, however. You don't want to push it when things are going good.

I stopped by Mr. Drake's room to give him my note. He read the note and looked up at me. Then he read it again.

"All right," he said, "I'll see you this afternoon."

I went back to my regular classroom. We were supposed to be handing in our lists of things we were grateful for. Mine was only half done. I was quickly trying to write things like "pencil," "shoe," "desk," "books," and "carpeting."

I almost made it to seventy. It was pretty close to lunch. I needed more time if I was going to finish it.

Melissa asked if we could have more time. She's such a Goody Two-shoes that the teacher was going to do it for sure.

I was going to write, "I'm grateful that Melissa is such a goody-goody so we got more time to do this assignment," but I didn't.

"Oh, all right," said my teacher, "you can hand it in after Thanksgiving break."

I went back to work and a wadded-up note appeared on my desk. I'm practically in the front of the class and it came from behind. I opened it up.

It said, "Hi."

That was it. "Hi."

I turned around to see who it was from. No one was looking at me. I had no idea who would send such a stupid note. How was I supposed to even answer it?

I didn't want to be distracted. I was trying to get done so I didn't have to take the list home to do. I was including everything. I had to include things like "windows" and "paper." I was desperate.

Melissa sits by me and I happened to look over at her paper. She had written, "I'm grateful for my teacher."

I could not believe her. She wrote it in huge

51

letters so it wouldn't be missed. Will she get an automatic *A*? I would guess so.

Not me, I was too busy being grateful for the bathroom tile and toothpaste. I didn't think to put down my teacher. You'd think one of these days I'd learn. I didn't add it to my list, either, because that would've been cheating and I'm not a cheater. The bell rang and I didn't get done.

Later, I stood in line with Bob to get lunch. She was bummed. They had a bunch of relatives coming and she had to spend the weekend sleeping in the attic with her brother.

She said, "It's creepy."

"Why do you have to sleep there?" I asked.

"The relatives get the beds," she replied.

"Yuck," I said. "Why don't *they* sleep in the attic?"

"They're too old," said Bob.

"Well, get this," I said. "I'm in the play this afternoon. Scott confessed and I'm not in trouble anymore."

"You're kidding," she said. "What are you going to do?"

"I'm going to be in the play," I answered.

"No," she said, "about Scott."

"Nothing," I said. "What should I do?"

"I mean," she said, "are you going to talk to him?"

"About what?"

"To thank him."

"No way," I said. "He's a creep."

"He could've not told the truth," Bob reasoned.

"Well, he could've not thrown the turkey, too," I said.

"I think you should be nice," said Bob.

"Please," I said. "No way."

Then out of the corner of my eye I saw him. He was looking at me. I tried not to look back. I poked Bob with my elbow.

"Ow!" she said.

"He's looking at me," I said.

"Where?" She started looking all around.

"Don't look," I whispered. "He's right over there by the door."

Bob looked right at him and waved. I could not believe it.

"What are you doing?" I asked.

"I'm just being friendly. You should try it sometime."

I said, "You are not my friend. He's a total geek. I can't stand him. Do not wave at him. He got me in trouble yesterday, including being sent to the principal's office. Do not wave at him; he'll throw something like a table at you and I'm not going to catch it this time."

10

We did our play in the afternoon. It was so ridiculous. Everyone was laughing.

First off, Mr. Drake wouldn't let us have the food, so we had to pretend. I mean, originally, we were pretending with the fake stuff. Without it, we were double pretending.

He said, "It'll show who the great actors are."

It didn't. It just showed that he was too chicken to bring that turkey out because he thought someone might throw it. I'm telling you, the food was the only good thing about the play.

He wouldn't let the guys paint themselves, either. They looked stupid painted but at least it was something different to look at. Marcia wore a pink dress, what a surprise.

She said, "My mother told me I could."

I was grateful I didn't have her mother.

Jane and Emily bagged the high heels for their run through the forest, but one of the Native

Americans stepped on the end of Emily's cape, which was really long, and when he did he practically strangled her. She got really upset and started crying. Mr. Drake tried to just smile.

He kept saying so everyone in the world could hear, "Just keep going."

During the crowd scene around the Thanksgiving feast table that didn't have any food on it (while we were having to pretend it did), I whispered to Bob, "We look like starving nuns."

"I know," she whispered back.

"I'm never being in a play again."

She said, "You said that last time when you had to play the cow in *Jack and the Beanstalk*."

"Don't remind me," I said.

"You were a great cow," Bob said.

"Don't push it, Bob," I said.

With relief we sang the last song and the audience clapped.

"Very creative," Mr. Drake said.

"Very stupid," I whispered to Bob.

"You said it," she answered.

I could look out over the school and in the back I saw you-know-who. He was standing by the door. He was clapping and whistling with his fingers in his mouth.

What a punishment, I thought. He doesn't have to be embarrassed. It's not fair.

We got on the bus to go home. Luckily enough,

parents picked up their kids so I got a seat to myself. Booger almost tried to sit with me but he decided to sit with his friends.

I thought, Wow, tomorrow is Thanksgiving and everyone is coming to our house and my dad . . .

I remembered that I had all this stuff to do when I got home.

Great, I thought, it's the garage or the basement. I'll do the garage.

Booger beat me home from the bus stop and was getting into the car with Mom when I walked up to the door.

"Where are you going?" I asked.

My mother said, "Your dad forgot a few things. We're running to the store."

"Can I go?" I asked.

"No," said my mom. "Go in the house and start helping your dad."

As they were driving away I yelled, "I forgot to tell you I'm not in trouble anymore."

They didn't hear me. I went into the house.

"Dad," I yelled.

"Hi, Lizzie," he yelled back from the kitchen. "Change your clothes. We have major things to do."

"Dad," I said, "I'm not in trouble. I have a note from the principal."

"What?" he said coming out into the living room.

I handed him the note.

"Well, what do you know?" said my dad. "I guess you're sort of off the hook."

I smiled.

"See," I said, "you should believe me."

"Oh, Liz," he said, "I believe you. It's just that you have a small habit of attracting trouble."

He ruffled my hair and hugged me hard.

"Change your clothes," he said, "and get something to eat. We have so much to do, it's incredible."

"Okay," I said.

I changed and made myself a peanut butter and honey sandwich.

My dad came in and said, "I just went by your room. You'd better start there."

"Dad," I said, "no one will go in there. I'll just close the door."

"No way," he said. "Clean it up."

I shoved my sandwich in my mouth and grabbed a glass of apple juice. I thought I was going to choke.

"Don't leave the glass in your room," he said.

I started cleaning my room. Right off I found two math papers under my bed that I had looked for last week. I wondered if I could still hand them in.

I also found one of Booger's socks.

What is his sock doing here? I wondered.

He probably put it there just to make me crazy.

I rolled it up tight, knowing that having touched it, I would have to disinfect my hands and probably my whole body. I walked down the hall and threw it as hard as I could into his room.

The doorbell rang.

My dad yelled from the kitchen, "Liz, can you get it? I'm in the middle of this cooking thing."

"Sure," I yelled back.

Even though I'd just gotten started, I would've done anything to take a break.

The doorbell rang again.

"I'm coming!" I yelled.

I ran to the door and opened it. There was no one there. However, there was a large cardboard box.

I dragged it into the living room. My dad came out of the kitchen.

"How's the cooking?" I said.

He only shook his head. It wasn't a good sign. He said, "Who was at the door?"

"No one," I said. "It was just this package."

"Hmmm," he said, "what do we have here?"

The box said all over it, CAUTION. RALPH'S GIANT TURKEY. Open at your own risk.

"It's our turkey decoration," he said.

"You're kidding," I said. "That thing Booger — I mean Booker — wanted us to buy?"

"Ya" — my dad nodded — "and it appears it's on time. I thought it was a joke."

Then the doorbell rang again.

"I'll get it," I said.

I opened the door and went into shock. It was Scott.

"Who is it?" said my dad.

I wanted to say, "No one. It's just another turkey."

11

My dad said, "Well, don't just stand there with the door open. Invite him in."

"He's just leaving," I said.

"No," Scott interrupted, "I'd like to come in if I could. I mean, if it's okay."

"Sure, it's okay," said my dad. "A friend of Lizzie's is always welcome here."

I wanted to kill my dad.

"I just came over to apologize," said Scott.

I nearly passed out. I could not believe how embarrassing this was.

"I wanted to tell Lizzie," he added, "that I was sorry I got her in trouble. I don't know why I threw the turkey at her. I just do things like that sometimes."

I was in shock before and now I was in total shock. I was in triple shock. What was I supposed to say?

"Okay," I said.

"Well isn't that nice of you," said my dad, "and what a difficult thing to do, too."

Scott and my dad were smiling at each other like idiots.

"Well," I said, "we've got a whole lot of stuff to do."

"Ya," said Scott, "I've got to go."

I went to open the door for him.

"Are you sure?" my dad said.

I could have killed him again.

"Ya, I've got to go," said Scott.

I felt like pushing him out the door.

"Well," said Scott, " 'bye and sorry and thanks."

"See you later." My dad waved and then blurted out, "What the hey?"

We all looked to the middle of the room where the turkey box was. It was moving. It looked like something was inside the box pushing the sides.

"What's in there?" I said.

"I don't know," my dad said, "but I think we'd better get it outside."

"I'll help," said Scott.

"We don't need any," I said.

The box jumped.

My dad went over to the box and pushed it with his foot. The box turned slightly. My dad jumped away.

"Do you think there's an animal in there?" I said.

"I hope not," said my dad, "but I don't know what else it could be."

"Someone playing a joke," I said. "Booger, are you in there? Is that you?"

"Booker is with your mother," said my dad. "You two watch out, I'll move it toward the door."

My dad went over to the box and reached down to grab it and move it. The box jumped three feet away from him. He went toward it again and it moved again. He ran and dove at it a third time but just as he almost touched it, it jumped out of his reach.

"I'm freaked," I said. "Dad, we'd better call the police or fire department or something."

"Well," my dad said.

"What if it's a bomb?" Scott said.

"It isn't a bomb," I said. "Bombs don't jump."

"Right," Scott agreed. "Well, what is it supposed to be?"

"A giant paper turkey," I answered.

"Gobble, gobble," said my dad, trying to make a joke out of it. "You two help me. We'll get it cornered."

"Dad," I pleaded, "I think this is a mistake. What if it's a snake?"

"Could be a cougar," Scott added.

"Let's get it outside." My dad looked at the two of us. "C'mon help me. It'll be okay."

"Famous last words," I wanted to say.

The three of us tried to corner the turkey box.

It kept jumping out of our reach. We had it pinned over by the kitchen but it jumped so hard it opened the swinging kitchen door and went in there.

We followed it but it was moving so fast we had to run. It was zooming through the house. It was like a speed-racer cardboard box.

We started chasing it upstairs but then it reached the top step and turned around.

"Get out of the way!" my dad yelled.

We turned around, too, and ran back down the stairs. The box was right behind us. I was jumping three steps at a time.

The box must have hit my dad. It hit him hard enough that he fell. He fell on top of Scott, who fell on me. It was dominoes and I was on the bottom.

"Oomph," I groaned as the box sailed over us.

"Sorry," said Scott.

"You two okay?" my dad asked.

"Ya," I said. "Now can we call the police?"

"Okay, okay," my dad agreed. "I'll call."

The box was back in the middle of our living room again.

"Well" — I turned to Scott — "you can go home now."

"Not on your life," said Scott.

My dad picked up the phone and started to dial.

"Dad!" I screamed. "The box is opening."

The top flaps popped open. My dad, for some

unknown reason, set the phone back down on the receiver.

"Dad, call the police," I said, but it was like he was hypnotized. He couldn't take his eyes off the box.

None of us could. It was coming apart. I mean, it was unfolding very carefully and very slowly like it had a motor. It was like the box was mechanical.

The final flap came down and there it was. It was a turkey. It was a paper turkey. It wasn't giant. It was just a normal paper turkey. It was folded out ready to decorate some Thanksgiving table.

It had one of those stupid-looking paper turkey heads. Its body and tail feathers were honeycomb-looking stuff made of yellow tissue paper. It was actually a normal-looking paper decoration turkey.

We all started laughing nervously.

"Gobble, gobble," my dad said again.

Why did he say that? Why did he say anything? The turkey turned its head like it heard him.

12

"**D**id that turkey's head just move?" I said.

"I don't think so," said my dad.

"Maybe it's a battery-operated paper turkey," said Scott.

"You're insane," I said.

"Liz," my dad warned.

We stood at least ten feet from the turkey and stared at it for awhile.

My dad said laughingly, "I guess it's done. Man, what a trick. That was amazing. I wonder how they do that."

"Dad?" I asked.

"What Liz?"

"It's moving," I said.

"It's — it's — " Scott stammered, "unfolding."

It was. It was unfolding and at a rapid pace. It was like every inch of it was unfolding a flap and then that flap was unfolding and then another and then another.

"I guess this is how it gets giant?" my dad asked.

"I don't like this," I said.

It was very weird. It kept looking like a turkey but it was still unfolding. It was getting taller and wider by the second.

Scott turned to my dad. "How big do you think it is?"

My dad said, "I thought it was about four feet tall a few seconds ago but it's bigger than that now."

It was continuing to grow.

"I wonder when it stops," I said, raising my voice.

The tissue paper was starting to make a bunch of noise.

"You know what?" my dad asked.

"What?" I yelled.

"I think I'd better get it outside," he said.

It was practically six feet tall.

"How?" said Scott.

"I don't know," said my dad.

"Did it just move the couch?" I asked.

My dad said, "I'll grab it and push it out the sliding glass door to the deck. You guys go open the door and pull it through."

Scott and I went around the turkey toward the door.

"The head is hitting the ceiling," said Scott.

"This is so crazy," I said. "Why did Booger have

to order this stupid thing? My mother is going to have a fit."

I couldn't see my dad anymore.

"Are you at the door?" I heard him say.

"Yes!" we both yelled.

"Is it open?" he yelled back.

"I'm opening it now," I said. "The lock is stuck."

"Tell me when it's open," he said.

I fiddled with the lock. It was really stuck. I couldn't make it budge.

"Let me try," said Scott.

"Excuse me?" I said. "I live here. I know how to unlock the doors."

"Well," he said, "you're not getting it unlocked."

"Who are you?" I said. "A locksmith?"

Then I felt the crunch of tissue paper on my back. The turkey was right up against us and the head was folded over and lying flat against the ceiling.

"Hurry, Liz!" yelled my dad. "I wonder if there are any directions to this thing. I wonder how you fold it up."

I pulled hard on the latch. I beat on it. I heard a lamp crash to the floor as the turkey spread to the rest of the room.

Then bully Scott reached over and undid the latch.

"Ya," I said, "after I loosened it."

Then before we could get the door open, it

seemed like the turkey exploded. With one huge crunch sound it totally expanded, pinning Scott and me with our faces smashed into the sliding glass doors. From outside, it must have been a real attractive sight.

"I can't move," I said.

"Neither can I," said Scott.

"Dad!" I screamed.

"What?" he yelled back.

"We're trapped. We can't move."

"Hang on," he said. "I'm coming through. I think I see a pathway through the honeycomb things."

Fear struck me.

"Don't, Dad," I yelled.

Then I heard my dad or someone yell, "*Yo-o-o-o-o-o-o-o-o-o-o-o.*"

It sounded very far away. It sounded like someone who was jumping off a very tall cliff or going down a very long slide. I knew he was in the same room, but it sounded like he was a mile away.

The turkey was quiet. I thought it was done unfolding.

"Dad?" I yelled, trying to move my smashed face.

There wasn't an answer.

"Where is your dad?" said Scott.

"How would I know?" I said. "Where is yours?"

He didn't answer me.

"Scott?" I said.

He didn't answer me.

"Scott, are you okay?" I said.

There still wasn't an answer.

I tried to turn my head the other direction. That dang honeycomb stuff was just digging into my head and back.

"Good grief," I said, practically breaking my nose to look at where Scott should have been.

"Scott?" I said.

He wasn't there. A minute ago we were right next to each other and now he wasn't there.

"Scott, where are you?" I screamed like a crazy person, which if you know me, I'm not, but on this occasion I was seriously considering it. Besides, I was getting a headache and I thought for sure my nose was going to bleed.

He didn't answer. I did hear something, though. It was a crinkly noise. It was getting louder.

Oh no, I thought, it's not going to get bigger.

"Dad!" I yelled with all my might.

13

I felt like I couldn't breathe. I actually could breathe but everything was so close, I didn't feel like I could.

Yellow-colored tissue paper was around me on all sides. I was encased in one of the turkey honeycombs.

This is beyond strange, I thought. I know what Christmas presents must feel like.

I pushed on the paper to feel the sliding glass door. I couldn't feel it through the paper.

I thought, Hadn't I just been pressed up against the door? Maybe I got sucked toward the center of the turkey.

I tried to get my bearings. The paper was too close all around me. I was starting to hyperventilate a little so I tried to calm down and think good thoughts.

I didn't have any good thoughts.

Where's Dad? I thought.

I pushed on the paper again.

"I could tear this," I said.

I pushed harder. It ripped. It didn't rip easily but it ripped.

I tore pieces away and now my encased area was at least a little larger.

Which direction should I go? I wondered.

I thought way too long about it.

You idiot, I thought, you're in your living room. What difference does it make?

I started ripping like crazy. I even got a rhythm going. It was kind of "rip, rip, stamp, stamp." Don't expect to hear it on the radio very soon.

Every now and then I'd stop and yell for my dad.

"Dad, oh, Dad. Where are you?"

At least the ripping was keeping me calm and I felt like I could breathe again. I ripped and stamped some more and then I ripped and stamped again. I tried karate kicking for awhile but it made me too tired.

It felt like at least fifteen minutes went by.

I should be to a wall or a window or a door by now, I thought.

The only thing I could figure is that I was going in a circle but I'd still have to bump into some furniture or something.

"I'm never decorating for anything again," I said.

I ripped some more. I looked down at my watch. It wasn't moving. It was stopped.

"Dang it," I said, "that was a brand-new battery."

For a minute I thought I heard something. It was muffled but it sounded like, "rip, rip, stamp, stamp." I either had an echo or someone else was doing what I was.

"Dad!" I yelled.

The sound had stopped.

I kept going. I felt like I was in the jungle or something. I needed a machete. A knife of any kind would have been great.

"I'm glad there aren't any snakes," I said.

I wondered if I could maybe run real hard against the paper and burst through. You know, like when a basketball team runs through a frame with paper over it. The paper usually says something brilliant like WIN.

I backed up a few steps and started to take a running leap through the tissue paper. I ran and leapt. I mean, I threw myself like a combo ninja warrior, professional hurdler, football player, and ballet dancer. I had my legs sort of split and my hands were in fists. My eyes were closed and my mouth was wide open.

"Hi-i-i-i-i-i Ya!" I yelled.

I sailed through the paper like it was nothing. It was like toilet paper. I landed on the ground sort of in the position I flew through the air in. I was positive I'd ripped all the muscles in my legs and that my ankles were broken.

I kept my eyes closed and rolled over onto my back. I brought my knees up to my chest and I put my arms around them.

"Not smart, Lizzie," I said.

"You said it," someone answered.

I looked around and realized I'd jumped through the paper into what looked like a dimly lit room. I looked for where I burst through the tissue paper and I couldn't find it.

"What happened to our living room?" I asked.

I seemed to be in a large room but it was almost like a cave or a dungeon. It had stone walls with large arches and thick solid-looking wood doors under them. The room was lit by torches high up on the walls.

"I'm totally confused," said the voice.

"Who are you?" I asked. I was scared.

A hand reached down from out of the shadows to pull me to my feet.

"It's just me," said the voice, "Scott."

"Oh," I said, almost glad to see him. "Where are we?"

"You tell me and we'll both know," said Scott.

"How'd you get here?" I asked.

"I don't really know," said Scott. "One second I had my face smashed against the sliding glass door in your living room and then the next minute I was here."

"Really?" I asked.

"Ya," he said. "How'd you get here?"

73

"I jumped through the turkey tissue-paper stuff," I said, acting like he was so stupid because he saw me.

"No," he said. "How'd you get to the door and how did you get it open?"

"What door?" I said.

"That one," he said, pointing to one of the heavy wooden doors. "I've been trying to get it open for an hour but I need help."

"Honest," I said. "I did not come through that door. I ripped tissue paper and jumped through it till I got here."

"You came through that door," said Scott, "and I saw you. I don't think it's funny. You guys have the weirdest house in the world and I just want to go home. I won't tell anyone. Just tell me how to get back outside so I can go home."

"This isn't our house," I said. "How can you think this is our house?"

"I don't know what to think," Scott said. "I've been down here for hours. I thought you guys had kidnapped me and all I want to do is go home."

I thought he was going to cry.

I was mad. "Great," I said, "that's two of us. Lead the way."

14

"Listen," I said to Scott, "that is the most ridiculous thing I've ever heard of. Why would we want to kidnap *you*?"

"I don't know," said Scott.

"Exactly."

"Maybe," he said, "because you're still mad at me."

"Please," I smirked. "I don't have people kidnapped just because I don't like them."

"Oh," he said quietly.

For some unknown weird reason I think I hurt his feelings. I looked around.

"I wonder where we are?" I said.

"You really don't know?" said Scott.

"No," I answered. "I really know but I'm not going to tell you. What do you think? Do you think I'm having a good time? My hands are covered with paper cuts and they're probably going to get infected and have to be amputated and you think I'm having a good time."

"I'm confused," said Scott.

"You said it," I agreed.

"I wonder what time it is?" Scott asked.

"My watch stopped," I said.

"So did mine," said Scott.

We both said in unison, "Weird."

"Let me think," I said, which I know was stupid but don't you sometimes say something dumb because you don't know what to do or say? I do.

"About what?" said Scott.

"About how we got here," I said.

"Where is here?" said Scott.

Without thinking I said, "Inside the turkey."

"How could we be inside the turkey?" said Scott.

He was getting on my nerves.

"I don't know," I said. "If I knew I'd have it all figured out and I wouldn't have to think about it, would I?"

"Geez," said Scott, "why don't you have a crab sandwich for lunch."

"Well you're not exactly any help," I said.

We both looked out over the room.

"What's that smell?" I said, holding my nose and looking at Scott.

"It wasn't me," said Scott.

"I didn't say it was."

"I'm getting out of here," said Scott.

He started walking over to the nearest door. He pulled on it. It didn't budge.

He jogged over to the next door.

I said, "I think we should think this through before we do something stupid we're going to regret."

He was totally irritating. He ignored me. He was yanking on the next door. It wouldn't budge, either.

He ran to the next door, which was getting quite a ways from me.

I talked to myself. "This is just like him. He's doing something when he should be thinking about it first. If there was a turkey here, he'd throw it at me. Thank goodness there isn't a bomb in here or he'd decide to blow the place up."

He hollered at me, "Liz, come help. I think we can get this one open."

I walked slowly over to the door.

"And what," I asked, "do we do if we open it up?"

"Maybe," he said, "we can get out of here."

"Well," I said, "maybe there's a monster behind that door and we'll let him out."

He finally stopped to think.

"I guess we have to take that chance," Scott decided.

I said, "I knew you were going to say that."

Then the lights grew dimmer. One of the torches burned out. Scott and I looked at each other in panic.

We both grabbed the handle on the door and

pulled with all our might. It was moving. Another torch burned out. We pulled harder.

The door was open. It wasn't open wide but it was open.

Scott said, "I'll hold it and you squeeze through."

"No way," I said. "Talk about a tight squeeze and I can't see anything in there. It's pitch-black."

"If you're chicken, then hold the door and I'll go," said Scott.

I wanted to slug him. I took a deep breath, let it out, and mashed myself through the crack we'd opened up. Scott followed me and just as he pulled his arm through, the door slammed shut.

We were standing in the pitch-dark. I mean, I could see nothing. I hate standing in the pitch-dark. I pushed on the door like crazy.

"Open up," I said.

I could feel Scott next to me, pushing.

"It's no use," he said, giving up.

"No use!" I yelled. "I can't believe you talked me into this. Now what are we supposed to do?"

"I don't know," said Scott.

"I don't know?" I asked.

"That's right," said Scott, "I don't know."

"Terrific," I said, "just terrific."

We stood in the dark in silence.

I then heard Scott move away.

"Where are you going?" I asked.

"Well," he reasoned, "we can't stay here."

"Sure we can," I said. "We'll be missed. We'll stay here and someone will see our picture on TV and come looking for us."

Scott laughed.

"It's not funny," I said.

"Ya," he said, "it is. You're funny."

"No I'm not," I said but I started to laugh. "I'm not laughing, I must be hysterical."

"Come on," he said. "Hang on to me and we'll see where this tunnel or room goes. We can feel the wall."

"You feel the wall."

"Okay," said Scott. "You hang on to the back of my shirt. Don't rip it. It's my favorite."

I didn't want to, but I grabbed on to his shirt and we started walking.

"It's a rock wall," he said. "Watch out for the hanging snakes."

"What!" I screamed.

"Just kidding," said Scott.

I jerked on his shirt.

"Hey, you're choking me," he said.

"No kidding," I said.

We walked awhile.

"You guys didn't kidnap me, did you?" he asked.

"You got that one right," I answered.

"And somehow or somewhere we're inside that turkey thing, but we should be in your living room," he said.

"Gosh!" I said. "You get straight A's."

"Are we in your basement?" he asked.

"Our basement is weird but it isn't this weird," I said.

"Look out," said Scott, "I've hit some stairs."

"Up?" I asked hopefully.

"Down."

"I was afraid you'd say that," I said.

15

We slowly went down twelve steps. I counted them. Then we were on the flat again. Before the floor had been hard like it was a rock surface. Now it felt softer, like dirt.

"I feel like I'm in a dungeon," I said.

"Ya," is all Scott said.

"I wonder where my dad is?" I said.

Scott asked, "Do you hear something?"

We stopped. I could only hear my own breathing. Then something went past us at a very fast rate. You could hear it breathing. It sounded large and animal-like.

I swear I could feel hot breath on my skin. I could smell wet fur. I would've screamed but it happened too fast.

We stood frozen.

After several minutes I ventured, "What was that?"

"Ya," said Scott, "like I know."

"Do you think it's coming back?" I asked.

"How would I know?" Scott snapped at me.

"I'm just scared," I said. "You don't have to yell at me."

"Ya, like I'm not scared," said Scott.

We didn't say anything for awhile.

We kept going, sort of shuffling along until I heard Scott yell, "Ow!"

I then plowed into his back and fell down. I got up. I had no idea how many spiders were on the ground — or rats or snakes.

"What's wrong?" I whispered.

"We're at the end," said Scott. "Why are you whispering?"

"What do you mean?" I said loudly. "Where are you?"

"I'm trying to find out if there's anywhere else to go," said Scott.

"Is there?"

"No," said Scott. "Well, there might be. This wall feels like wood and it might be a door, if I can find a handle . . ."

I heard a thud and a plunk and then a creak. Then a door opened. There was some light.

"You did it," I said.

We walked through the door.

"Weren't we just here?" I asked.

As far as I could tell, we were right back where we had started. We were back in the large room with the torches on the rock walls, the arches, and the big wood doors.

"How?" said Scott.

"Maybe it's a different room," I said.

"How could we ever tell?" Scott asked.

"I don't know," I said. I felt like crying.

"But we went down some stairs," said Scott.

"But the path could have been going uphill," I added.

"That gradual, so we wouldn't notice it?" said Scott.

"How can you tell in the dark?" I groaned.

"Did we come out the same door we came in?" asked Scott.

"How should I know?" I answered.

Scott sat down on the floor for just a second. The door behind him slammed shut and he jumped to his feet.

"Yo!" he yelled.

I lost it and started hollering for my dad. "Dad! Oh, Dad! Dad! Dad!"

Scott looked at me like I was a total nerd.

He said, "Will you stop?"

I stopped. "What?"

"We just have to keep trying different doors. We'll mark them so we know which ones we've gone through," said Scott.

"Why?" I asked.

"Because," he said.

"Because why?" I asked.

"Because, what else are we going to do?"

He had me.

"I don't want to walk through the dark anymore," I said.

"Then we'll get one of the torches," said Scott.

"One that isn't burned out," I said.

We looked at the remaining torches. There were six. Two had already burned out.

Then, for fun, I counted the doors. There were sixteen.

"Uh, Scott," I said, "there are sixteen doors."

"We've already done at least one," said Scott.

"Uh, Scott, then there are fifteen doors."

"We just have to get started," he said all chipper.

I hate it when people are chipper when they should be totally depressed.

"We've got to move," said Scott. "We can't just sit here."

"We're standing," I said. "How are we going to get a torch? They're too high. I don't know about you, but I can't jump that high."

He ran and jumped up trying to reach a torch. He slammed into the wall instead. He stood back holding his shoulder and looked up at the torch.

"I guess jumping is out," he said. "Here, stand on my shoulders and you can reach it."

"No way."

"Okay," he said, "I'll stand on yours."

"Very funny."

"Well?"

"Well?"

"Your shoulders or mine?"

"This is so irritating," I said. "How do I get up there?"

He stood with his face to the wall.

"I'll bend over a little and you just step on my back and then get on my shoulders and then I'll straighten up," he said.

"Right," I said flatly.

"You've got to try," he said.

One of the other torches went out.

"Fine," I said.

I put my knee on his back.

"How much do you weigh?" he asked.

"Shut up," I said. "This was your big idea."

I put my hands on the wall and put my other foot near his shoulder. It was working.

He said, "I'm dying, hurry up."

"I'm trying to concentrate so I don't fall," I said.

"Do it faster."

I slowly stood up with both feet on his shoulders. I tried to reach the base of the torch but I was like two inches too short. Scott was still slightly bent over.

"You've got to stand up more," I said.

"Like I could," he said.

"You've got to try," I said.

He inched his feet closer to the wall and I felt him straightening himself upward.

"Is that enough?" he asked.

I grabbed the base of the torch and pulled it out of its holder.

"I've got it," I said.

"Jump," he said.

"What?" I asked.

"Jump quick or I'm going to collapse and we'll be burned to death."

I didn't know what to do.

"Jump!" he screamed.

It was great. I did a backward jump off of Scott's shoulders with a flaming torch. I should be in the circus.

16

"We're in a maze," I said. "We're like in a labyrinth."

"Ya, right," said Scott. "Just help me with this door."

"I suppose you don't care that there might be a Minotaur down here with us and we may be walking into his trap," I said.

"You're crazy," Scott said.

"Well," I said, "tell me what isn't crazy?"

Using our torch and marking the doors with charcoal from the torch, we had explored two more of the doors. Actually, we had explored four of the doors because each door we entered just ended up at one of the other doors that, when opened, brought us back to the main room.

"I think we have enough torch left to do one more door," said Scott.

"I get to pick the door," I said.

"No way."

"Why not?"

"Because," said Scott.

"You picked all the last ones," I said, "and they went nowhere."

"We don't have time. I'll pick unless you'd like to figure out how to get another torch," said Scott.

"Then do I get to stand on your head again and get another?" I asked, making the huge mistake of laughing.

"I don't know why this is so funny," said Scott. "I don't think this is all that funny. I mean, what if we die down here?"

"Sorry," I said. "I was trying to keep our spirits up or something."

"Well, don't," said Scott.

"Sorry," I said again. "I'll try not to inconvenience you by breathing."

"So?" said Scott.

"So what?" I said.

"So if I hadn't come over to your dumb house to say I was sorry, I wouldn't be down here," said Scott.

"If," I said, just kind of yelling, "you hadn't thrown that turkey at me in the first place, this would have never happened. You would never have had to come over to my house, so you wouldn't be here!"

"So maybe you wish I wasn't even here," said Scott. "Maybe you'd like to do this all by yourself.

Well go ahead. You know so much, go ahead without me."

"Ya, I wish you weren't here . . ." I said and I was going to add that I wished I wasn't there either, but he didn't give me a chance.

"You're making me mad," said Scott.

"What do you mean?" I said. "All I did was laugh. Excuse me."

"Do you want the torch?" asked Scott.

"What do you mean?" I said.

"Do you want the torch or do I get it?" answered Scott.

"Scott," was all I said.

"Fine," he said, shoving the torch toward me and practically burning my hair, "you take it."

"This is so stupid," I said.

He was running off, picking a door to go through.

"Scott," I said again, going toward him, "this is dumb. Let's just go together."

"Forget it," he said. "You didn't want me down here so just do it by yourself. Good luck."

"That's not what I meant," I said.

He glared at me.

"Okay, so it's what I said but I really didn't mean it."

He looked down at the floor.

"Gee whiz, I didn't know you were so stubborn," I said.

"Fine," he said and started pulling on a door.

"Let me help," I said.

"Please stand back," he said. "I can do it myself. I don't need any help. I'm too stubborn."

I could've screamed. I was just going to let him go. I was just going to stand there and let him go. It wasn't like he wouldn't be back. Then I started feeling like maybe this was the correct door, if there was one, and maybe I should go with him.

"Scott," I said, "I'm sorry. I didn't mean it. You're not stubborn. Okay, you're kind of stubborn but you're not stupid, and I'm actually kind of glad that you are here because it makes it more fun at least, even though we can't find a way out."

"Really?" said Scott cautiously.

I smiled at him. It practically cracked my face. I don't think I'd ever smiled at a boy before.

He didn't exactly smile back.

"Okay, sort of," I said. "So it's dumb for us to fight. Right? I'm glad you're here. I'm glad you're stubborn because people think I'm kind of stubborn, too. So let's shake hands."

I stuck out my hand.

The creep wiped his nose with his hand and then stuck it out to me. Like I wanted to shake it then. I don't believe boys. What could I do?

I shook his hand and reminded myself to wash it really good later. I looked down at my hand to casually see if there was anything on it. There was. My hand had gold stuff on it.

"What's this?" I said, looking at my hand.

"Looks like gold stuff," said Scott.

"No kidding," I said. "Where did it come from and is it toxic waste?"

"I don't know," said Scott, looking at his hands. "It's all over mine, too."

We both turned and looked at the door that Scott had been pulling on. I walked over and touched the door handle. I looked at my finger. It was covered with something gold.

"The gold thread," I screamed. "This is the door out. I know it. It's the gold thread. You know, Ariadne got Theseus out of the labyrinth by giving him a golden thread. This is our golden thread."

"That's crazy," said Scott.

I thought for a minute. It was crazy. "It sounded good," I said.

"This is not a labyrinth," said Scott. "We're somewhere in your basement."

"Excuse me," I said. "I know my basement. This is not my basement. So stop saying this is my basement. This could be a labyrinth. I mean it could possibly be a labyrinth."

"Ya, right," said Scott, "and it could have a Minotaur in it, too."

Right then we heard something from across the

room. Someone or something was pushing on one of the doors. It was butting against it.

"What's that?" I whispered.

"I don't know," Scott whispered back.

"What if it's a Minotaur?" I said.

"We run like crazy," said Scott.

"Where to?" I said, staring at the door.

17

We heard a "grunt" and a "thud." It echoed down through the room. Then we heard the same sequence a second time.

Then there was a pause, like whatever it was needed to get all its strength together. Suddenly we heard an explosive "bam" against the door and then a "creak" as it opened. I fully expected a half-man and half-bull to come through the door.

What do you say to a Minotaur — *toro*? I didn't know if I was going to scream or not. I took a huge breath just in case.

Something came out of the door. It looked big enough to be a half-and-half bull and man. I couldn't tell for sure because it was dark down in that part of the room. Then I think it spotted us.

Instinctively I grabbed Scott's arm or maybe he grabbed mine. Anyway, it happened that fast. I was too scared to remember. I could hear my heart beating two miles away or it could have been Scott's heart.

I thought, Great, I'm going to die down here, wherever I am, with Scott. We'll probably have a joint funeral. All my friends will be wondering what I was doing here with him.

"Lizzie?" the thing said. It sounded like a cross between a question and a command.

Oh no, I thought. The thing knows my name. This whole situation has been a setup. What do I do?

It was just a trace nicer. "Lizzie? Scott?"

Then it dawned on me. I sort of knew that voice. I kind of knew that shape.

"Dad?" I said, running toward him.

I hugged him like a total big baby and almost started crying. I was really happy to see him. Then it felt like something was wrong.

He acted like he didn't know what to do. He put his hands on my shoulders but he didn't hug me back. That wasn't like my dad.

"Dad?" I said. "Are you okay?"

"Of course," said my dad briskly.

I looked at him closely. He looked almost normal. Something was different about him, though. I tried to just toss it off because of the bizarre situation but I had a bad feeling.

"Dad," I said, "where are we?"

"Here," he said.

I tried to laugh because I wanted to assume it was a joke.

"Are you two okay?" he asked with a flat empty voice.

"Ya," I said.

"How about you, Scott?" asked my dad again, almost sounding like a recording.

"Okay, I guess," said Scott.

"I'm really glad to see you two," said Dad, but it didn't sound like my dad. He sounded mad. It was weird because he was saying nice things but he sounded mad.

"I'm glad to see you, too," I said. "But, Dad, you sound funny."

He didn't say anything to me.

"Sir?" said Scott.

"Call him Phil, Scott," I said.

"No," said my dad, "call me sir."

My dad hates to be called sir. He hates it. He says he hates it as much as wearing a tie.

"Yes, Phil — I mean, sir — I mean, sorry," said Scott. "Do you know where we are?"

"Of course," said my dad, acting like we were idiots because we didn't know.

"Where?" asked Scott.

"The turkey is big," said my dad. "I was in the room next door. I heard your voices in here so I tried to get in. The doors are heavy."

My dad sounded so strange, I wanted to whisper to Scott, "We've been abducted by aliens."

My dad said, "I really had to push on the door."

"We know," I said. "We heard you."

Scott was laughing.

"What's so funny?" asked my dad.

"It's just that," said Scott, "Lizzie thought you were a monster."

I wanted to strangle that creep.

I gave Scott a mean look and said, "I just thought you were totally lost forever so I'm really glad to see you."

"Well, sir," said Scott, "I thought we must be in your basement."

"This isn't our basement," I said.

My dad just stopped for a second and then said quietly, "This is my basement."

I thought this was getting beyond a little weird. There was a noise across the room. We looked over at the door. It was closing on its own.

"Well," said Scott, "I guess we can check off that door. Were there a lot of other doors in that room?"

"Yes," said my dad, "many."

"Great," both Scott and I said, totally disappointed.

"Why?" asked my dad.

"We've been trying some of the doors in here but they just lead back to this room," said Scott.

"You have?" my dad said, kind of mad. He paused. "That's dangerous," he said. "You shouldn't have done that. You should have waited for me."

I said, "We wanted to, Dad. We just didn't know what else to do."

"Ya," said Scott.

I said, trying to sound very grown-up, "You always tell me to use my best judgment and to listen to myself and trust myself in doing what is right and, well, I didn't really think this was totally right but . . ."

I was getting a sick feeling looking at my dad.

"Kids," he barked at us.

"What?" I said after I jumped fifty feet.

"No matter whose idea it was, don't do it again. You wait for orders," said my dad.

"Ya," said Scott.

"I know," I said. Then I whispered to Scott, "He's usually not this bossy."

"We need a new torch," said my dad.

I started to tell him how I stood on Scott's shoulders to get the last one but my dad had gone across the room and it looked like he just climbed the wall like he knew exactly where to put his feet. He came back with the torch.

"Boy," said Scott, "I didn't see any foot things to climb the wall."

"You didn't look," said my dad. "Okay, let's go through here." He pointed at another door, not the one with the gold on it.

"Lizzie thinks this door with the gold on the handle will lead us out," said Scott, almost like he was making fun of me.

"She does?" said my dad. "We're going through this one. It's better."

"Okay," said Scott.

Scott and my dad pulled on the door. What was I supposed to do? I finally pushed my way in and tried to help.

"We don't need your help, Elizabeth," my dad said.

"Sorry," I said.

They opened the door.

"The stairs go . . . down," Scott said, kind of pulling away from the door.

"That's for sure," I said, looking in. The stairs went straight down, steeply.

Scott said, "Should I go first?"

"No," said my dad, "you'd better follow me."

Then I noticed something. My dad was carrying the torch and I could see my shadow and I could see Scott's shadow but I couldn't see my dad's shadow. The way the light was, my dad's shadow should've been on the wall next to ours. It wasn't.

Every cell in my brain said, Don't go with him. It's my dad, I thought. No, it's not, I answered myself.

I grabbed Scott. "That's not my dad," I whispered.

"Come on, now," said the man who wasn't my dad.

18

My dad, or whoever this was who looked like my dad, started to lead us down the stairs. Of course Scott was right behind him. I hung back just a little.

My dad was looking weird to me. He seemed like he was taller and his ears were kind of big. His teeth seemed bigger.

They were steep, steep stairs and they looked a little shiny, like there was moisture on them.

Great, I thought, they're slick.

We followed him for just a short while and the stairs took a sharp turn, still downward. From looking at the shape of the wall it was like they were starting to spiral down. There was water dripping and I could hear it hitting a pool or something.

I was feeling more and more uncomfortable. It felt like we were getting led somewhere bad. I felt like whoever this was had been here before.

The thing that looked like my dad went around the corner. I grabbed Scott's arm.

"What?" Scott said.

I put my hand over his mouth to make him shut up. I pulled us against the wet wall.

I whispered, "Don't say anything. We have to get out of here. That's not my dad."

I took my hand off his mouth.

"Are you sure?" he whispered. "How do you know?"

"I know," I said. "Trust me, let's get out of here."

We turned around and started up the stairs, trying to see with just the dim light still coming in through the open door.

The thing said, "Scott, Elizabeth, are you coming?"

We didn't say anything. We tried to hurry. The stones were so slippery it felt like trying to skate upstairs.

"Run," said Scott.

Whatever it was, now was following us.

"Stop!" it roared.

We were at the top. The door was still open. We ran through it. Both of us pulling and pushing tried to shut it.

The thing was bounding up the stairs toward us. I don't know if it was the reflection of the torch or not, but it looked even less like my dad. Its eyes were on fire and it was on all fours. It looked very big and very hairy. It was snorting like an animal. My dad wouldn't think of snorting.

We slammed the door in its face. We could hear it pounding and trying to get out.

"That's not your dad?" said Scott.

"Please," I said.

We were holding the door.

"Now what?" said Scott.

"We go through the gold door," I said.

"Without a light?" said Scott.

The door was being butted against.

"Yes," I said. "Let's just go *now*."

We ran over to the gold door. I checked the handle to make sure it was the right door. It was.

Both of us pulled on the door using more strength than we ever thought we could've had. We got it open just a crack. We could hear the thing bamming away at the other door.

We got the gold door open about eight inches.

"We can make it," I said.

"You go first," said Scott. "I'll hold it."

The thing burst into the room. It had thrown down the torch and was running madly around. It was almost like it couldn't see us.

I squeezed through the door opening. I pushed against it so Scott could get through.

"Hurry," I said.

He squeezed through and we tried to pull the door shut. We really didn't need to. It slammed shut on its own. We turned from the door.

"Is it sort of light in here or are my eyes doing weird things in the dark?" I asked Scott.

"No," he said, "it is sort of light."

"It's a good sign," I said.

We could make out stairs. They were going up. They were narrower than the other passages we had been through. We started up and went as fast as we could. It wasn't very fast. I was afraid of falling. It wasn't that light.

"Is it getting more light or is it me?" I asked.

"It's you," Scott said. "We're making a corner."

It was definitely lighter. We turned another corner and there we were. My instincts had been right. We were, well, we were somewhere.

We were back in the honeycomb paper stuff but there was sort of a pathway through it.

"Do you think we're back in your living room?" Scott asked.

"I don't know anything anymore," I said.

"Who was that guy?" Scott said. "What did he want?"

"I'm telling you I don't know. I only know he wasn't my dad and he was bad."

"Well," he said, "if that's true, you saved my life."

He looked at me kind of weird.

"I was saving mine," I said, "and we'd better not stand here. He's probably after us."

We followed the path till we came to a dead end. We kept looking behind us.

"I guess it's time to rip," I said.

We started tearing through the paper but we couldn't tell what direction to go in. It was impossible to see where we were. Then I had a brilliant idea.

"Scott," I said, "what if I stood on your shoulders and ripped a hole on top so I could see where we are?"

"What?" he said.

"You heard me," I said.

He thought about it. "Okay," said Scott. "Don't break my back, and when I say 'get off,' you have to."

He got down on one knee and I climbed up and sat on his shoulders. He stood up. Then, taking his hands, I stood up one foot at a time.

I was bumping my head against the tissue paper above me. Scott was, let's say, wobbly.

"Steady, Scott."

"I'm trying."

I reached up with one fist and punched a pretty good hole. Then I stood up straighter and looked out. I thought I was going to fall off.

"Where are we?" said Scott.

"I don't know."

"What do you see?" said Scott.

"You don't want to know."

"What?" he screamed.

"Well," I said, "I see blue sky."

"And?" asked Scott.

"For miles all the way around, all I can see is this dang yellow paper honeycomb stuff. There's like an ocean of it."

"You're kidding," said Scott.

"I wish," I said.

"Where does it stop?" asked Scott.

I squinted my eyes to see the edge. I thought I saw it. Then I was sure I saw it. I saw the edge and it was moving.

"I see it," I said, "and it's doing something."

"What?" said Scott. "Hurry, I can't do this much longer."

"It seems to be . . ." I said, pausing to look. I then screamed, "Collapsing!"

It was. It was doing it at an incredible rate. It was folding in on itself. It was doing it at about a mile a second and I would swear that it looked like the sky was collapsing with it.

"We're going to be crushed!" I yelled.

I jumped off Scott in panic and practically killed myself. I landed against the paper and bounced back onto Scott.

"What did you do that for?" asked Scott.

"We've got to run," I said. "We've got to get back to the basement."

"No way," said Scott.

Then we could hear the sound of the paper collapsing. It was gaining momentum every second. It was deafening. It was like a million pieces of paper being crumpled up at once.

"Run!" I screamed as loud as I could.

We turned and ran as fast as we could back toward the stairs. I fell down like four times I was going so fast.

"Where are the stairs? Where are the stairs?" I kept repeating.

It was too late. Suddenly there was a huge burst of wind blasting us from all sides. I couldn't breathe. My lungs couldn't get any air. I couldn't scream. I couldn't move. I was frozen.

19

I woke up, I guess I woke up, or I came to, on our living room floor. I looked over and my real dad, I hoped, was lying on the couch. Scott was on the floor across the room by the window.

"Where's the turkey?" I said but no one heard me.

I quickly scanned the area. It wasn't in the living room. Then I saw it.

It was in the dining room. Sitting in the middle of the dining room table. I got up and walked toward it. Scott was waking up.

"Where are you going?" he said.

"I'm going to slaughter a turkey," I said.

"What?"

By then, I had the turkey in my hands and was ripping it apart.

Scott said, "Let me help."

He grabbed a slab and ripped it into little tiny pieces. Then we each wadded up our turkey, threw it on the ground, and jumped all over it. We pulverized it. We made bologna out of it.

I said, "Now we take it outside and put it in the trash."

"Burn it," said Scott.

Then my mother and Booger walked in the door. My dad woke up.

"Honey," she said to my dad, "what are you doing?"

"Wow," he said, "I must have fallen asleep. What a dream I had."

"Phil," she said, "I can't believe you slept. I left you with all this stuff that has to be done."

"Sorry," said my dad. "I don't know what got into me. I didn't think I was that tired. I don't remember even lying down."

My mom was ticked. I was elated. I ran over and hugged my dad.

It was him for sure. I could tell. He acted like my dad. He hugged me back.

"Hi, Dad," I said like a complete goon.

"Hi, Liz." He grinned.

My mother said to me, "Elizabeth, who's your friend?"

Booger, the idiot, said, "It's Scott and he's her boyfriend."

My mother said, "Booker, carry the groceries into the kitchen, please."

"Mom," I said, "it's Scott from school."

"Hi," said Scott weakly.

Booger, who wasn't carrying in the groceries, said, "What is in your hand, Lizzie?"

"Nothing," I said.

Scott started to talk but I accidentally on purpose kicked him.

"Ouch," he said. "It's nothing."

Then Booger happened to spy the turkey box in the corner by the front door.

"Did we get something?" he asked, going over to read it.

Who bothered to teach him to read?

"My turkey came," he said. "Who opened it? They shouldn't have."

"Did we get a turkey in a box?" my dad said. He didn't remember.

Moving away from me so I couldn't kick him, Scott said, "It sort of opened itself."

"Where is it?" asked Booger.

"Uh," I said.

Then Scott said, "It came damaged."

"Right," I said. "It came this way."

I held out my hand. Booger was major disappointed. I halfway felt bad.

"Sorry, Booger — I mean, Booker," I said.

"Oh, well," he said, "I'll just have to make one. It will be even more giant than that one was going to be."

"I don't think so," I whispered to Scott.

He started laughing.

I wanted to say, "Way to go. Get me in trouble again."

Booger went running off to make a turkey.

"Booker," my mother said, "the groceries."

"Make Lizzie," he said, already upstairs. "Do we have any brown paper?"

"I'll do it," I said. "I'll carry in the groceries."

It gave me a chance to get rid of the turkey.

"I'll help," said Scott.

"No, you won't," I said. "You have to go home, remember?"

"Oh, ya," he said. "But I can help you carry in the groceries."

"Isn't that nice," my mom said. "Scott, you wouldn't believe the kind of day I've had. Trying to get ready for Thanksgiving and, Phil, I can't believe I left and you took a nap."

"I've had an interesting day myself," said Scott.

"Mom," I said. "I'm not in trouble at school."

"That's nice, honey," she said, heading for the kitchen.

We walked out the door to the garage.

"We got lost in a giant paper turkey," Scott said, trying to get a grip on reality.

"We did," I said, trying to help him. "We got lost in a giant paper turkey."

"Okay," he said, "really?"

I put the turkey in our garbage can. That had to do for now.

"Stay!" I commanded it.

Scott laughed.

We picked up the grocery bags and carried them to the back door and into the kitchen. My mom was still telling my dad how upset she was that he had taken a nap.

"Thanks, kids," she said.

Then for some stupid reason I said, "Thank you."

20

Thanksgiving went okay. We got everything done. My dad helped me vacuum the basement and sweep the garage. My mom spent most of the time cooking everything my dad didn't get around to and then some.

My dad made a dish called Turnip Surprise. It wasn't a surprise to me that no one ate it.

Everyone said, "What's this?" and then when they were told, they all took half a teaspoon just to be polite.

Everyone gave my dad a bad time because we were having a turkey. My dad didn't eat any, though.

"Do you know what they feed those things?" he said back.

"No, and I don't want to," said my uncle Greg.

Crazy Aunt Mary called at the last minute and said she wasn't coming. I was disappointed. My dad was, too. My mother was trying to act disappointed but I think she was secretly grateful.

She said, "It just won't be Thanksgiving without dogs howling in the garage, will it?"

Crazy Aunt Mary had decided to go to Reno with some friends at the last minute.

She told my mom, "I'll call when I win my first million."

My grandmother went "Humpf" when my mother told her what Crazy Aunt Mary had said.

"Oh, by the way," Crazy Aunt Mary had said, "I've met a new man. His name is Ralph and he's absolutely magical."

"I'll bet," said my dad.

"What does he do?" I asked my mom.

"I didn't ask," she said.

"We don't want to know," my dad said. "He probably trains snakes."

"I just wondered," I said.

My mother kept telling everyone that Booger had made the decorations.

She said, "He did them all by himself."

It wasn't like he'd just discovered a new planet. I was grateful, though, that she told them. That way they didn't wonder whether I made them or not.

He made a turkey out of a paper bag. It didn't look like a turkey, it looked like a paper bag with newspaper in it. He used pink and blue paper for the tail feathers. It looked very weird.

I told him, too.

"Mom," he said.

"It looks stupid," I said. "I'm sorry. I thought you wanted me to tell the truth."

"Elizabeth," she said, "please be appropriate and nice. It won't kill you."

Everyone ate too much. Booger ate enough olives that he probably is going to turn into one. He kept putting them on all his fingers, like they were fingernails. It looked disgusting. I hate olives.

Everyone tried to help with the dishes, which is a disaster because you get all these people in the kitchen and my mother goes crazy and it takes twice as long to do them. I had to dry. It was so crowded I ended up drying dishes with my dad on the back porch. There were three pies left over.

Then we played board games. Someone got pumpkin pie on half the money in my Monopoly game. I swear it was Booger but he denied it.

I went outside twice to check the garbage can and make sure the turkey was still there. The first time it was. The second time it was gone.

I looked for it in the garage. I looked for the box it came in. It had been flattened and put with the recycling stuff. The turkey wasn't there, either.

I freaked out a little.

"Maybe someone is just playing a joke," I told myself.

I was grateful when everyone left. However, it meant that we had to reclean the house the next day.

We did. It was boring.

Booger wanted to keep his turkey decoration. I threw it across the room to him. He made a huge deal out of it and I got in trouble.

I tried to get my mom to go out and start Christmas shopping.

She said, "Elizabeth, you've got to be kidding."

"No," I said.

"No way," said my mom.

"Why?" I asked.

She wouldn't tell me. She went back to studying and writing papers. I started looking at Christmas catalogs. I marked all the stuff I wanted for Christmas.

I felt stupid because I kept thinking about Scott. I was going to call him up and see if he wanted to ride bikes or play or something. I didn't, though.

The following Monday, when I got back to school, I handed in my gratitude list. I finally had a hundred things.

The teacher said, "Now wasn't that fun?"

We all answered, "No."

Later in the day she called me up to her desk and asked me about the last thing on my list.

"I'm just a little confused," she said. "I was just wondering why you put that on your list?"

She pointed to Scott's name at the bottom of my list.

"It has to do with turkeys," I explained. "There are some big ones out there and you have to be careful. It sometimes helps to have friends."

She looked at me and laughed.

"People aren't always what they seem like at first," I said.

"Lizzie, I'm impressed," she said.

"Thanks."